Visiting Aunt Sylvia's

A Maine Adventure

by HEATHER AUSTIN

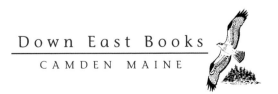
Down East Books

CAMDEN MAINE

Dust-jacket and interior design by Harrah Lord, Yellow House Studio

Printed in China

6   5   4   3   2   1

ISBN 0-89272-523-0

Library of Congress Control Number 2002108300

DOWN EAST BOOKS
Camden, Maine

For catalog information and book orders, call
1-800-685-7962, or visit www. downeastbooks. com

Dedication

Dedicated to the true Sylvia, my dear friend and inspiration,
and to the memory of Ronald Sands for believing in me.

Special thanks to my young friends
Paige and Joshua.

Fall

FALL at Aunt Sylvia's spreads out over the mountains like a colorful patchwork quilt. She lives deep in the woods of Maine, on a hill she calls Paradise Knoll. We take long walks and watch deer eating from apple trees. A flock of honking Canada geese flies over our heads. Aunt Sylvia says they are on vacation, too, but they will come back in the spring.

At her cabin we help cut firewood for the winter. I stack the kindling, and my brother, Toby, gathers twigs. Afterward we harvest wild grapes. They have seeds and taste bitter, but Aunt Sylvia makes them into sweet grape jelly.

The next day we dig for a precious stone called tourmaline at a forgotten quarry. Tourmaline is mostly black, but we find some pieces that are pink and even green.

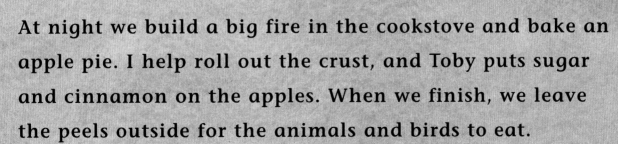

At night we build a big fire in the cookstove and bake an apple pie. I help roll out the crust, and Toby puts sugar and cinnamon on the apples. When we finish, we leave the peels outside for the animals and birds to eat.

On the last day of our visit, I make a leaf mobile to hang in my window at home. Now I will always have fall at Aunt Sylvia's.

Winter

WINTER at Aunt Sylvia's is sparkling white. The trees
are bare, and the mountains are covered with a blanket
of snow. Now we ski though the forest, and Aunt
Sylvia wears snowshoes. We see rabbit tracks
and a fox carrying home a squirrel for her
dinner. Aunt Sylvia says this is a hard
time of year for the animals.

Back at the cabin, we warm up with cocoa. Toby and I coat pine cones with peanut butter then roll them in birdseed. Outside, we hang the cones on tree branches for the chickadees.

For our supper, we eat baked beans and biscuits with molasses. Dad makes his specialty: coleslaw. The fireplace crackles as we toast marshmallows and listen to Aunt Sylvia play the piano.

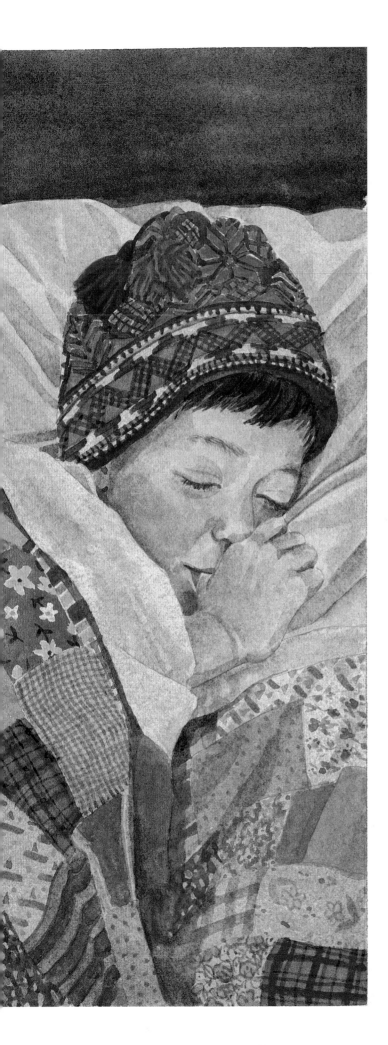

The sleeping loft gets so cold in the winter that we have to wear hats to bed. Luckily for me, the cat, Maria-Theresa, keeps me cozy warm.

Just before we have to leave, I find a bright blue jay feather and stick it in my hatband. Now I will always have winter at Aunt Sylvia's.

Spring

SPRING at Aunt Sylvia's is a busy time of year. There are lots of things to do outdoors when the snow melts away. Toby and I help Aunt Sylvia plant marigolds around her garden patch. She says these flowers keep away the bugs but not the rabbits. Dad and mom repair a leak in the cabin roof while we sweep the deck. Aunt Sylvia makes us lunch, and we have a picnic in the sunshine.

Afterward, we go for a walk. Everyone wears boots because the ground is soft and mushy. It's mud season in Maine! There are lots of biting blackflies, so we only stay long enough to pick a basket of fiddleheads, which are little ferns that haven't opened yet. Aunt Sylvia cooks them with butter and vinegar, and we eat them all.

The next morning Aunt Sylvia wakes us up early and says she has a surprise for us. She takes us to the tool shed, where Maria-Theresa is sleeping with two baby kittens! Toby and I get to choose their names. They are tiny and soft, and their eyes are still closed.

It rains in the afternoon, so we stay indoors and everyone except Toby plays Monopoly. He falls asleep with the kittens.

When the sun finally comes out, it makes a rainbow over the mountains, just as we are leaving for home. Aunt Sylvia gives us a loaf of freshly baked bread and a glass prism. She says that if we hang the prism in a window, it will make rainbows at our house, too. Now I will always have spring at Aunt Sylvia's.

Summer

SUMMER at Aunt Sylvia's is bursting with life. The weather is so nice that we decide to hike to Step Falls for a swim. The water is very cold, but we dry quickly on the warm granite rocks. Mom doesn't swim, so she falls asleep and gets a sunburn.

On our way back to Paradise Knoll, we buy corn on the cob and lobsters for supper. Aunt Sylvia lights candles on the deck, where we eat and tell stories. Mom rubs aloe on her sunburn, and dad helps Toby and me catch fireflies.

Afterward, I go look for Aunt Sylvia. I find her in the hammock, watching the dark sky. She shows me certain stars and tells me their names. I hear a noise, and Aunt Sylvia points to a raccoon that is eating the leftover corncobs we put out for the animals. He is fat and has funny little paws.

The next morning, we go to a flea market. Mom and dad buy an old rocking chair, and a nice lady gives Toby and me a bag of marbles. There is lots of neat stuff for us to play with.

In the afternoon, we collect wildflowers in the woods, and Aunt Sylvia weaves us crowns of daisies to wear. She shows us where to find blackberries and lets us look at birds through her binoculars. Later, Aunt Sylvia shows us how to save our flowers by pressing them between the pages of a book. Now I will always have summer at Aunt Sylvia's.